W0232971

PENGUIN BOOKS
DEV & SIMRAN

Eunice de Souza (1940–2017) was born in Pune where she grew up. She graduated from the University of Bombay, did her postgraduate work at Marquette University in the US and later obtained a doctorate for her thesis on Indian poetry and criticism from the University of Bombay. She taught English literature at St. Xavier's College, Mumbai, and was head of the department till she retired. There she organized poetry readings and was later involved in setting up of the well-known literary festival 'Ithaka'.

She was the author of several books of poems. Her groundbreaking book of poems *Fix* was published in 1979, followed by *Women in Dutch Painting* (1988), *Ways of Belonging* (1990) and *Learn from the Almond Leaf* (2016). She also wrote two novels—*Dangerlok* (2001) and *Dev and Simran* (2003)—several books for children, and edited several poetry anthologies, the last of which, *These My Words: The Penguin Book of Indian Poetry* (2012), she co-edited with Melanie Silgardo. In the last several years of her life she brought all the weight of her knowledge to her much-loved weekly *Mumbai Mirror* column on reading and literature which she wrote right to the end.

BOOKS BY THE SAME AUTHOR

A Necklace of Skulls
Dangerlok

EUNICE DE SOUZA

Dev & Simran

a novel

PENGUIN BOOKS

An imprint of Penguin Random House

PENGUIN BOOKS

USA | Canada | UK | Ireland | Australia
New Zealand | India | South Africa | China | Singapore

Penguin Books is part of the Penguin Random House group of companies
whose addresses can be found at global.penguinrandomhouse.com

Published by Penguin Random House India Pvt. Ltd
4th Floor, Capital Tower 1, MG Road,
Gurugram 122 002, Haryana, India

First published by Penguin Books India 2003
This edition published 2019

Copyright © Melanie Silgardo 2019

All rights reserved

10 9 8 7 6 5 4

ISBN 9780143029588

This is a work of fiction. Names, characters, places and incidents are either the
product of the author's imagination or are used fictitiously and any resemblance
to any actual person, living or dead, events or locales is entirely coincidental.

Typeset in Amerigo BT by InoSoft Systems, New Delhi

Printed at Repro India Limited

This book is sold subject to the condition that it shall not, by way of trade
or otherwise, be lent, resold, hired out, or otherwise circulated without the
publisher's prior consent in any form of binding or cover other than that in
which it is published and without a similar condition including this condition
being imposed on the subsequent purchaser.

www.penguin.co.in

This is a legitimate digitally printed version of the book and therefore might not
have certain extra finishing on the cover.

For Mena Müller and Jennifer Morton
In friendship

The imperfect is our paradise.

'The Poems of Our Climate'
Wallace Stevens

Acknowledgements

With thanks to Melanie Silgardo who read the manuscript and Ravi Singh and Poulomi Chatterjee, editors.

Prologue

DYING. A MELODRAMATIC thing to happen to an ordinary guy. Or so Dev thought. He had been feeling he should say something profound to Simran, something significant, that summed up their life and relationship. All he could think of was where his investment papers were and what to do about the insurance.

Now Sim tells him they're all in the next room or outside in the corridor: Maya, Ved, Sim's mother, Dev's mother, Rishad and Vimi, aunts, uncles, cousins. The lot. The doctor won't let them into the ICU.

Sim says, 'Ved says "Cheers! And one for the road!" ' She suddenly becomes aware of how that sounds; she stops.

The Sister comes in and tells Dev, 'You really must rest.'

Sim says, 'Right. I'll go and make a call or two.'

Dev looks at the Sister. Her head seems to swing from side to side like a pendulum.

'Call the doctor,' the Sister says, 'his pulse is dropping rapidly.'

Maya

WHATEVER THE SITUATION—Husband/Wife with the
Sulks, Mother with Smile of Silent Suffering, Boss
with Indigestion—Dev had one word of advice: I.G.
Ignore. Alternatively: Avoid. Poor Dev, to wake up
one morning with some difficulty in breathing, and
to be dead of blood cancer three days later. I had
only a split second with him in the ICU; the doctors
were afraid of infections. I touched his hand and
said, 'Dev.' I could not bring myself to smile and say,
'Dev.' I could not bring myself to smile and say, 'I.G.,
Dev.'

Before they carried the bier away, Simran put his
favourite soft pillow under his head, and we stood
around chatting, as if it were just another evening at
their home, with Dev presiding at the little bar of
which he was so proud.

∞

'Deblina,' I said to my assistant at the Women's
Studies Unit, 'if I hear one more person saying "The
Good Die Young" or some such, I shall scream.'

'They have to say something,' Deblina said.

'They don't have to say anything. "Time Heals".
God! The man's barely dead. And Time *doesn't*
heal.'

'I don't know about that. I've no experience.'

'Sim and I bought that bar for him. It wasn't really
a bar, just a rather lovely, delicate cupboard. And we
asked the guy to stick it on an old carved table. It
turned out well, didn't it?'

'How's Sim?'

'Inundated with relatives.'

'Sheesh.'

⠀⠀⠀⠀⠀⠀⠀⠀⠀⠀⠀⠀⠀⠀∾

I remember a time when Dev and Sim were going
through one of their bad patches. 'The problem is,'
I said confidently, 'that you guys don't talk things
through enough.' So I hauled them both off to the
Sea Lounge and said, 'Okay, now let's talk.' Dev
squirmed and Sim looked in an interested way at
people passing by. Then we ordered coffee and chilli
toast and left in half an hour or so.

I should have learned a thing or two from that, but
a while later when Sim stormed and raved and said
Dev had called her stupid, I said, 'Of course you're
not stupid. He's stupid. In fact, he's a pompous ass.'

Sim turned on me and said, 'What the hell do you mean? He's a friend of yours, isn't he?' After that we didn't talk to each other for a week.

Tricky.

☙

I envied Sim her little certainties. She'd say, 'Dev likes to go down and fiddle with the car in the mornings,' and trivial as it was, it would make me wish I knew people in that way. I didn't. Reading a great deal of literature didn't seem to help. Most books explain everything to you, or at least the old-fashioned ones I love do. Why on earth did X marry Y? A sentence three pages long and with plenty of parentheses would tell me the exact reason. German men prefer prostitutes who are pregnant. Some book would explain that too, even if I didn't want to know. Books explain too much, too much that is no help at all.

'You're too bookish, Maya,' Sim would say.

Sim never reads a book if she can help it. 'Intelligence,' she says, 'isn't the same as common sense.'

Sim's right, of course. In the early days at the Unit I had these very bookish ideas of how to solve problems. I would tell vacillating women to take a stand. But they couldn't, otherwise they wouldn't have been vacillating in the first place. I would tell women who were being beaten to leave home. What they did was leave the Women's Studies Unit. Where could they go given the price of flats in Bombay? Stapling circulars was the only useful thing I seemed to do at the end of it!

&

'I'm writing about Eve,' I said to Simran once.

'Eve? Eve who?'

'Eve, as in Adam and.'

'Oh, that Eve. Whatever for?'

'A column on The New Woman.'

'Sweet child. Write about me. Change of name to protect, etc.'

'You're not The New Woman.'

'I'm not? I've put up with a lot of shit and stuck around.'

'Sati Savitri Simran.'

'It takes guts to stick around and try to make it work.'

'Tell me more.'

'Well, one year into marriage and no grandchildren prattling and cutofying for ma-in-law, so off we go to a gynaec and I swear, Maya, his prodding and poking wasn't just medical.'

'Ugh!'

'Very ugh! Anyway, I said, that's it babes. No more visits to the miracle man.'

'What did Dev say?'

'Dev didn't say. His mama said. His two older sisters said. His maternal aunt said.'

'Didn't you ever feel like quitting?'

'Sweet child. All guys have mamas.'

'Too true.'

'So write about me: Strong Woman Protagonist.'

'I'll think about it.'

෴

'Fuck' is a useful little word. Years ago I'd never have dreamed of using it. But one day in a coffee house I ran into a lawyer I vaguely remembered. He came up to my table and said, apropos of goodness knows what, 'So you're the great Maya who teaches women to hate men! You're a pervert.' I was startled, but I looked at him and said. 'Fuck off.' Amazing. He crumpled and walked away. Later I remembered who he was. He'd defended a man whose battered wife had come to me for some legal help.

After that the f-word and the b-words had come easily.

There's a lovely Wallace Stevens line which expresses what I've learned: 'The imperfect is our paradise.' No perfect husbands. No perfect wives. No perfect life. No perfect death. No perfect world. No perfect lawyers. What to do?

Bumble on.

∞

I remember quoting one of my favourite P.G. Wodehouse lines to Dev: 'He rushed at her and gathered her in his arms. She rushed at him and was gathered.' Dev said he had an even better one, and it was. 'He gazed at her fondly, like a cow gazing at a turnip.'

No. Strum and drang wasn't his style. 'Grand passions leave you feeling damn silly' was his little profundity. 'I just listen,' Dev said, 'then I do what I like.'

The very thought of all those conversations I had had with various bods about 'our relationship' still makes me cringe. I suspect I bored the pants off many a lover. Literally. They probably took me to bed just to stop me talking!

'Won't do,' Dev had said. 'Can't go around with your tongue hanging out. It worries guys.'

'If it's all so casual, why bother?' I had said.

'I don't know,' he said.

The next time I was at Dev and Sim's, I took along one of my favourite Shakespeare sonnets to show them. 'When my mistress swears she's made of truth/ I do believe her though I know she lies . . .'

'That's Shakespeare?' said Dev who never read much. 'Sounds like a sensible fellow.' He fixed me a drink and was then lost to cricket on TV for the rest of the evening.

But Sim said to me, 'If your anybody lied, you would want to know why.'

Yes I would. I don't like things which are unclear, unfinished.

৪৩

Is it death one minds, or the regrets it leaves you with? A woman I know wept for days because she had been too tired to make her mother a pudding she liked, and that night her mother had died. I haven't asked Sim about regrets. I'm not sure I can.

She'll tell me if she wants to. I must be growing up, I think. Finally. Something of Dev, dear non-reading, cricket-watching Dev, has rubbed off after all.

About two years ago, Sim had rung up early one morning, early for her, that is. 'Dev and I are taking a gentle trip to the jewellers,' she said.

'Whatever for? You've enough jewellery to decorate an elephant.'

'We're celebrating,' she said, 'I'm over the worst.'

'The worst?'

'I'm pregnant,' she said.

'Oops. Do you want it?'

'I don't know. But I'm going to keep it.'

'Dev thrilled?'

'Well, he's going round with a sort of modest smile.'

'And mother-in-law?'

'Fuck mother-in-law.'

'I don't think I want to.'

'Har har har.'

'I'll knit you some booties. Blue or pink?'

'I don't know. I think I'd rather it was a surprise.'

'Oh well then, I'll make them purple with yellow lines and green spots.'

Peter is giving one of his dinners this evening and I have promised to go. I mean, it was all arranged a month ago, before all this Dev thing happened. Peter was amazingly decent about it and said not to come if I didn't feel up to it, but it doesn't seem fair, what with him having to find another female at the last minute. I know I'll regret it.

∞

I find myself seated next to a youngish man with a goatee, and I turn to him even though I haven't the slightest desire to speak to him. 'What do you do?' I ask with great originality.

'I write,' he says.

And what does he write, I wonder. Letters? Birthday card greetings? It turns out he writes advertising copy. 'Fascinating,' I say, and turn with relief to the man on the other side who is a banker and talk about the weather.

'Nick,' Peter says addressing the banker, 'the lovely lady you are talking to is a feminist.' He winks at me as he says that.

The banker's soup spoon stops midway to his mouth. 'Down with men, what!' says the goatee.

'Ze Asian women are so passive and so wize,' says an unidentified nutter sitting opposite me, French from the sound of it. 'Zey do not make ze mistakes we do.'

'Actually,' I begin, but the conversation has drifted back to the problems of Microsoft, so I stare at my plate, unwilling to deal with the banker or the goatee.

'Don't hurry off,' says Peter as he hands me a liqueur. 'I want to talk about my unhappy childhood.'

'Your mother didn't love you enough.'

'No one loves me enough.'

'Where did you find this lot?' I ask after the last guest has left.

'They're on the circuit so I have to see them.'

'How can you stand it?'

'It gets a bit wearying, I admit.' He laughs. 'Goatee got your goat, did he?'

'It's disconcerting, that's all. You suddenly feel that the things you feel and do don't make sense to heaps of people. You have to go home and start trying to make sense of it all over again.'

Peter offers to drop me home, but I say I'll take a cab. 'Thanks Maya,' he says, and gives me a hug.

I don't deserve him.

Peter is easy and amusing. Dev liked him. But Dev could be very literal, and Peter seldom is. I remember

Sim telling me a funny story once, funny and typical. She was reading a column by one of these society women who thinks of herself as a 'woman's woman'. Apparently after reading one of her books, two women waited outside her hotel room all night and then rang the bell at 6.30 a.m. to say she had changed their lives.

'Why didn't they just set the alarm for 5.00 a.m.?' Dev said.

It was not so amusing for Sim in less impersonal matters, this, shall we say, literalness. Sim would come back after a weekend spent with her parents and Dev would look up from his bridge game or the cricket match on TV and say 'Hi! Good weekend?' and go right on doing whatever he was doing. 'Can't he manage a hug at least?' she would complain. Dev would say, 'What's the big deal? We're together, aren't we?' Then she'd say, 'Of course we are, but that's not the point, is it?' And he'd say, 'If that's not the point, what is?'

She took to joking about it. 'At least you don't snore,' she would say, 'or slurp your tea.' 'I never slurp my tea,' Dev would say indignantly.

Sim even bought him a book called *Hollywood Husbands*. 'What is it?' he said. 'My birthday or something?'

Sim is just the opposite. If she knows you well she can tell what is going through your mind and she notices the slightest change of expression. It can be quite disconcerting to have a running commentary on your thoughts a split second after you've thought them. In fact, it can be maddening, an imposition, an invasion of privacy.

But she wasn't always that sharp. I didn't know Sim when she had first come to Bombay after her marriage. She used to laugh later about how naïve she had been. When salesmen or saleswomen came to the door, she said, she would end up buying stuff she didn't want, either because they were persuasive, or because they seemed so bad at their jobs that she bought stuff just to cheer them up. She ended up with five frying pans, three gas lighters, and a pair of identical clocks. The salesman had said they could only be bought in pairs.

Sometimes, if it was a woman, she would invite her in and make a cup of tea.

Once it was a pair of salesmen with some liquid cleaning stuff for jewellery. She took off the silver chain she was wearing and placed it in a saucer. They poured some of the liquid into it and told her the longer the necklace stayed in the liquid, the brighter it would get. She didn't want it very bright and removed it after a few minutes. Then one of the salesmen said, 'Don't you have any gold?' It was the expression on his face that suddenly made her wary. 'No,' she said, 'I don't.' He looked very crestfallen, but she said thank you very much, would they please leave. Luckily, they did.

She didn't tell Dev, but she stopped opening the door to salesmen after that.

Sim adapted. She was good at adapting, better than me at any rate. Perhaps Dev realized this and was grateful.

ॐ

'Any more of your lot going bonkers?'

It was Simran. She hadn't called for weeks after she told me about the baby, but I was so glad to hear from her again that I did not complain. There would have been no point. She had 'good news' for the clan, after all. Indian families are like hurricanes and tidal waves, unstoppable, engulfing you in a sudden, overwhelming torrent.

'How's the baby doing, Sim?'

'He's got too many of my ma-in-law's genes, Maya. He's given me a kick or two.'

'He?'

'Whatever.'

When I told Peter that Sim had surfaced he said, 'How does she cope? I'd go mad.'

'She and Dev won't go mad. They have perfect social manners. But they grumble later. It annoys me.'

In fact, most of my friends annoy me: Deblina, brought up in Standard, affects a kind of Indian English, coming down hard on her consonants like a hammer on hard wood. Uday never keeps appointments, Loretta is always a day early or a day late for hers. Jan keeps falling in love with ex-cons and gamblers and wants you to love them. Amita billows in from London and tells you how you should treat servants and taxi-drivers, Sim smarms over everyone, and Dev always seemed most relaxed with his hearty one-time adda pals. Why does one stick around with these people? The answer to that 64,000 dollar question is, as always, I don't know.

෴

'Peter,' I said, 'I'm so glad you're not here to find yourself spiritually.'

'Heavens!' Peter said, 'What's brought that on?'

'I've just been reading yet another novel about a European who comes to Benaras to find himself.'

'I've had enough problems finding myself in Bombay.'

'You keep getting lost in your ten-bedroom flat?'

'Four bedrooms.'

'Actually, I'd like to go to Benaras, but not to find myself. You get wonderful wooden toys there. Someone once gave me a bug-eyed pink crocodile. I want some for Sim's kid.'

'Wooden toys?'

'He/she can play with them when she/he's older.'

'We'll go sometime. But I've got to go to London again for two weeks. Coming?'

'No. I've got a talk to prepare.'

'What shall I bring you?'

'Belgian chocolates.'

'So do I get a kiss?'

'You get a kiss.'

∞

Did I really once think that death made life more meaningful? If a flower didn't die it would be a plastic flower and we'd stop looking at it? I don't think I was stupid enough to actually say that to anyone. It's a very idiotic idea.

Sim's baby was a month old when she died. She had grey eyes like Sim's and soft, dark hair. They called her Sara. One day when Sim was visiting the neighbours and Dev was at work, one of the relatives' children rampaging around the house decided to pick up the baby. Another child made a grab for it shouting, 'My turn, my turn.' Between them they dropped the baby.

When Sim returned and was told, she nodded and shut her door. She sat around for hours doing nothing, and woke up screaming in the night. She and Dev hardly spoke to each other for months. In fact, neither said a word to anyone, the relatives in the house, their families, their friends. Their manners remained perfect. If you went over, they'd offer you tea or a drink. Dev would stand at his bar and say, 'A vodka with Schweppes?'

There are no pictures of Sara in the house.

ॐ

One of Sim's neighbours, a nineteen-year-old boy called Rishad, had taken a fancy to Dev and Sim and sometimes dropped in to keep Sim company or watch a match with Dev. Sim found his confidence impressive. He had had a steady girlfriend since he was fourteen, he said, and he intended to marry her even though her parents objected. 'Different community or some such shit,' he said.

He gave her the low-down on many of the neighbours, and a pretty low low-down it was. He had names for all of them: Podge and Stodge, Dimple and Pimple, Yakkity Yak, Vroom Vroom. He had no time for any of them but his mother called on them with sweets she had made and all that kind of thing. 'You know what mothers are,' he said.

He wasn't going to live with his parents after he married, and he certainly wouldn't go anywhere near hers. He was going to get a massively well-paid job, lots of perks, and buy a flat in Malabar Hill.

Sim looked forward to his visits. On the day the baby died, he came and banged on her door. 'It's me, Sim,' he said. 'Open up.'

'Have one,' he said, flashing his first-ever pack of cigarettes, 'I find it helps when I am down.'

ॐ

No Condolences. No priest. No rituals. No ceremonies. No flowers.

Nothing. Nada.

But what was the alternative? Dev flapping his wings, fine-tuning a harp?

Larkin got it right. 'Death is no different whined at than withstood.'

Of course, in spite of the 'No Condolences', relatives came, neighbours came, old servants came, friends came. Not like vultures anxious to gorge on the gory details or anything like that. Each felt the notice could not possibly apply to them.

Entering the room, I felt a moment of social doubt. Whom should I approach first? Sim, her mother, her mother-in-law?

Simran duly repeated the details, over and over again, like an actor in a play reciting lines that were not hers.

One of the relatives said, 'First Sara, and now this. Bad kismet.'

I could have hit her.

છ

These days Simran hardly seems to inhabit the world she moves in. Sometimes she stands at the window with a dish of food for the crows. There's not a crow in sight, but suddenly they seem to come at her from all directions, cawing and clawing.

This habit of feeding the crows started after Simran was amused by a crow who tapped at her window. Now there's a wide variety of them, one who twitches one of his wings in a kind of nervous tic, another who has a loud, hoarse, demanding caw. 'Patriarchal,' I call him.

The mother-in-law is bemused. Pure idleness is difficult to attain, she thinks, but Simran seems to have attained it. A baked dish, a few veggies, a spot of mild cleaning, an hour in the shower. Why doesn't she do something? It would get her out of herself.

The boy from the neighbour's comes by sometimes. 'We're going for a walk,' he says, so Simran goes for a walk. Sometimes he's silent, sometimes he natters. He doesn't know if she is listening or not, but he doesn't mind.

One day he told Simran she must get a computer. 'It's good fun,' he said.

'I'll never learn how to work it,' she said.

'My mother can't handle a remote,' he said, 'and even she's learned. No one can be that stupid.'

So Simran got herself a computer.

෩

Sim's friends (and she has many) are determined she should not have time to think. We take her out to lunch, tea, dinner, films, plays, parties. Sim comes along. She knows we mean well.

Two months after Dev's death, Sim gets all of us together to celebrate what would have been his fortieth birthday. She takes out the Black Label whisky he had kept for the occasion.

We raise a toast to Dev.

છ

Simran

'IN MY BEGINNING is my end', or is it 'in my end is my beginning'? Same difference. But I'm not what I was at the beginning. The beginning was an electric blue silk with a flaming orange border, bells on my ankles, a ring in my nose. I've kept that sari, a monument to youth and bad taste.

I had been shown to doctors, lawyers, engineers, captains and kings. The family were beginning to get edgy. I was sick and tired of smiling demurely. Then it was Dev's turn (that's who it turned out to be). He looked at the certificates I showed him, first in elocution, prize for drawing and embroidery, certificate for Best School Captain. He looked at them and smiled. He looked like a good-natured bear. The thought made me smile, a real smile. Encouraged, Dev said, 'Do you think you would like to marry me?' Suddenly tired of the whole business I said yes, and there I was in the middle of the whole shebang.

I can't believe that for the first few months I rarely called him by his name. One day he said, 'You can use my name, you know. No offence taken.' It was the same on our honeymoon. 'If you're embarrassed, we can put off the lights. Or just talk.'

I wanted him around, I wanted to know he wouldn't leave me. 'Leave you and go where?' he'd ask. He didn't sleep around, like some of the others in his 'gang' who suddenly appeared with teenies half their age. 'They are asking for trouble,' he'd say. I didn't know if he meant the teenies or his pals. Both presumably.

It was the mother who got on my nerves, don't ask me why. She didn't actually *do* anything offensive. But she'd wear this Patient Don't-Mind-Me Smile. It would have been easier to have a row.

If you asked her how she was she would always say, 'So so.' I mean, there was nothing wrong with her. I started to call her The So-and-So. In my mind, of course, but one day it slipped out and Dev wasn't amused.

My mother got on my nerves too. She kept asking if I had asked my mother-in-law's permission for this or that. I wanted to say, for God's sake don't turn me into a bloody doormat, you're a doormat, one in the family is enough. But there would have been no point. *She* would have started to wear the Patient Smile and that would have been too much.

The Bombay shops were so new and exciting I wanted to buy half the stuff I saw. I *did* buy half the stuff I saw. I wonder why I didn't want Dev to know.

He wouldn't have had a fit. I suppose the habit of concealment grows in a family living in not a very large space, like mine used to. I mean, everyone can hear every sniff and snort, you don't want them to read every thought as well. Maya says, entire families live in one-bedroom places, and when the sons marry, the balcony is walled up, or partitions put up in the living room. I don't know how they don't all kill each other. Maybe they do. The bai was saying that in one of the houses she works in there's a son who is a bit mental. The mother is so embarrassed (in this day and age!) she doesn't allow him out, and doesn't allow anyone to meet him. One day he locked the door and beat his mother with a stick. She screamed the place down till somebody called the police. She's still hobbling around. I'm not surprised he beat her. *I* would have beaten her.

Oh well, c'est la bloody vie.

છ

Dear Simran,

We've never met, but Dev and I were in school together. I saw the birthday remembrance in the

papers and was appalled by the tragic news. I hope
you will forgive the formality of a typed letter on
such an occasion, but I could never write straight on
blank paper.

The paper said 'No Condolences' so I will not
attempt to see you. But should you need any help,
please let me know. I'm at the High Court now, and
could help with any legal matters or investment
matters or even tax matters if you wished. It's the
least I can do for someone I remember with affection,
even though we lost touch a few years after school.

Please convey my condolences and those of my
wife to your family, and never forget we are there
for you.

Yours sincerely,
Asit Potnis

How kind, how really kind people are. They make
the heart thaw a little, at the outer edges, true, but
still thaw. With the letter from Dev's school friend,
the world had grown a little larger.

Dear Asit Potnis,

You have no idea how much your letter meant to me.
Will you bring along photographs of your schooldays
if you have any? Dev would never show me any of
his. He said with the kind of haircuts they had in
those days, he looked like a goon! Did you find
school as uninspiring as he did? All he remembered
was the Cricket XI of which he was a member, and
an exciting victory over a rival school. I'm afraid I
recognize only the cricketers I see in ads! I'm not a
real patriot.

Sincerely,
Simran

৪০

Dev and I once went to visit a friend's mother who
was in hospital. In the bed next to hers, separated
by a curtain, was a woman who let out hoarse shouts
every few minutes. The woman who was her
attendant made soothing noises. Suddenly the old
woman screamed, 'Why aren't my mother and father
coming to visit me?' The attendant said affectionately,
in Gujarati, that her mother and father could not

visit her—they had passed on a very long time ago. But the brother would come, she said, that evening, if not the next day. Sunday, after all, was a holiday.

Dev seemed very fidgety through all this. The patient we had come to visit said, 'The old lady makes a lot of noise.'

But when Dev and I got up to leave, Dev suddenly went across to the old woman. She was now sitting up in her bed, reading the papers, in a brief moment of lucidity. Dev said 'Get well soon', waved, and left. I was astounded. But the old lady waved back and said, 'I will.'

ଚ୬

Maya told me a strange story about some cousin of hers. She was an older relative, fifty-something. Her husband had a dozen complications. There were many times when he'd be close to death, the doctors would give up hope, the wife would prepare to mourn, and then he would recover. By the end of it, the wife was so drained she just wished he would die and get it over with. And yet, Maya says, she really loved her husband.

Love. Had my marriage to Dev been a Grand Passion? Hardly. I didn't really have a checklist for his qualities. He was familiar, comfy to be with most of the time. No, it wasn't a Grand Passion. It hardly ever was. Something more subtle perhaps, more insidious. The way he held his cigarette, a shade of blue against his skin, the talc all over the shower-room floor, the unemphatic voice.

And making love? A matter of affectionate tolerance sometimes, irritated tolerance once in a way when I was zapped, or he more interested in watching TV. Once in a long while, the Real Thing.

I can't face opening his wardrobe to give his things away. I've tried, but shut it quickly. It just seems too final. Carrying away the bier had not seemed final. It was a sound, like the other sounds I could hear, horns honking, the bell of a school nearby.

A quick and easy death. Easy for whom?

Time heals. Everyone says so. But it does not heal so much as just carry you away on a fast-flowing river, though you want to cling on to what you are leaving behind. Would a day come when Dev's face too would be a blur?

∽

Dear Dev,

I think I short-changed you. What did you feel, I wonder, when I toddled along for the honeymoon with rexine handbags to match my saris, and sunglasses with rhinestones? You didn't say anything. Words were not your thing. But when we came back to Bombay, you bought me a leather bag and glasses without rhinestones. That was an act of friendship I didn't recognize for what it was.

Sulks. That's what I had been good at. They could go on for days and make everyone uncomfortable. But you would fidget for a few minutes, and then forget about them, and talk to me as if nothing had happened. It was maddening!

You win after all, you irritating old coot.

Dev, come back.

ॐ

Dear Dev,

Today Maya showed me a strange little poem called 'Not Waving But Drowning'. It's by a woman called Stevie Smith and it's about missed signals. I thought for a long time about it. That's why relationships go wrong, don't they? Or can go wrong. Missed signals, confusing signals . . . I feel like an emotional cripple sometimes, learning to walk for the first time. And then there are times when I seem to do it too easily: work out what a person means, or could mean, or would mean if he/she knew how to say it. Too much imagination, you'd say. But I think the problem is that I have too little.

Maya hates it when I know what she is thinking. She's right. If I had imagination, I would not say out loud what she is thinking, even if I could guess. I should have remembered that with you.

Dear Dev, forgive me.

∞

Dear Dev,

Everyone is trying to find ways to get me away from myself. I haven't been there half the time. What you lived with was the tip of the iceberg. They have raised the Titanic, I'm digging around in my own sands, or whatever there is on the ocean floor. Is there a floor? Does no light ever get there? Even thinking about it is eerie. I feel like shutting all the windows and bolting all the doors and hiding under a dozen quilts and saying I'm safe, I'm safe.

Very often when I'm driving around or passing a restaurant that we used to like, I find myself in tears. Then there are times when I remember how you were generous but careful with money and how I would spend like there was no tomorrow. And now I'm grateful for the money. Maybe it's easier to cope with a car, a flat and all expenses paid. I don't know. The car had two flats the other day, but just near the house, so maybe you *are* looking after me.

A month or so ago the building shook a little. No, I mean it really shook. It wasn't just me having a thingie. Rishad told me all about it, not just quakes and tremors, but tectonic plates and things, pushing against each other, pushing up mountains and swallowing rivers. Vimi says it's ridiculous to build such tall buildings on such unstable land. If Rajan Towers must come down, I hope it's not in the middle of the night. I've taken to wearing your shirts as nighties.

The earth shifting and heaving under Bombay and people faffing about in Rajan Towers and other towers. There was a teacher in school who used to tell us how insignificant we all were. Just a speck on this planet which was a speck in a universe that was one of millions of universes. And now I hear (on one of the programmes I watch) that the universe is expanding, and one day the stars will be so far away that no light will reach the earth.

How do I believe in myself when all this is going on? How do I believe in Sim as Sim, and Maya as Maya, and Ved as Ved? How do I balance Sim and the universe?

෮ඏ

An e-mail from Deblina: 'At least you didn't have to have a silicon implant to please your man (or did you?). When the man goes, the implant goes too! One woman said she was glad to get rid of her husband, his smelly dog, and her bloody bosom.

What am I doing here? Having a good time, basically. The courses are good, teachers good-looking, room-mate can cook, and white wine is cheap. What more can you ask for?

I miss you guys. You haven't told me what Rishad and Vimi look like. How do they dress? Trendy? Ethnic? Ragbag? Does he have a cute butt?'

෮ඏ

And another one: 'You haven't noticed his butt? C'mon Sim, get a life. Vimi sounds alarmingly competent.'

ജ

Dear Dev,

Ved took me by surprise last evening when he said, 'Simi-jaan, if I weren't married already, I'd marry you.' I laughed, but he looked so miffed that I said, 'It's only because you took me by surprise.' I gave him a hug. He was upset already because his dog doesn't seem to be able to see very well any more. Sometimes, Ved says, he paws at the telephone wires as if he were trying to unearth or bury a bone. Even at the farmhouse he prefers to sit quietly in the sun instead of romping about as he used to begging for a game with a ball.

So much sadness in the world, Dev, and so little one can do about it. The daughter of the woman downstairs is terminally ill, and looks like a stick. I met the mother in the lift the other day and asked, 'How is she?' She answered in Hindi, 'Hai.' She's there. She touched my arm as we came out into the lobby.

I keep thinking I should make a will. Things happen so suddenly. But who would I leave things to? Ved took your ashtray (the blue pottery one) as a keepsake, Rishad took your cricket cap. And I've already told you about your shirts! I don't want to give your things away (the rest of the things, not the keepsakes), but somebody could use them.

I wake up feeling tired these days. Your mother says I should go for a walk when I feel that way. Vimi says a little mild pottering around the Handloom Fair isn't enough, even if I am loaded with parcels! I suppose they are right. Will power. That's what I need. Tiring, just to think about it!

৪০

Dear Dev,

Dropped in to see Maya after quite a long time. She was rather cool, but it may have been the effect of the woman visiting the Unit. She had such unmitigated views about everything. Something about middle-class feminism not being real feminism, and middle-class women spending their time playing bridge and exploiting their servants. Real problems, she said, were only to be found among the poor.

Maya quoted something I liked, 'Life is real wherever people are living it.' I forgot to ask her where it was from.

I told Maya later that I found the whole business confusing. I don't mean obvious things like wife-beating. I mean, when you meet ordinary guys, someone's father or brother, they don't seem wicked. You know what I mean, not more aggro than normally happens in a family. I mean, there's a woman and her daughter who scream at each other all the time somewhere downstairs.

If we are not talking about people, what are we talking about? Maya says laws about women, for one thing, and attitudes. She says I should try travelling alone in the north to understand what she means; living in Bombay we don't see the worst. Maya says she was travelling alone in the north by second class AC to some conference once, and in the middle of the night the guy in the adjoining berth was holding on to her foot! She thought she was imagining things and kicked! When she woke up, there was the guy, grey-haired and all, grinning at her. She sat up the rest of the night. Weird.

Maya admits she is confused too. There are so many questions to which she doesn't know the answers. She says we'll talk about it some time.

ॐ

Maya says not even birth, copulation and death are the same for us all. Where her bai lives, the lanes are so narrow that one would have to tie a corpse to the bier and bring it out sideways. Those people have no choice, they make do

I've been thinking about this, Dev. What choices did *you* have, cared for though you were? A quick and easy death, or one dragged out for a year or two with that chemotherapy. Which would you have wanted?

I hear of people who have been paralysed for ten years and can barely gurgle out a word, or slowly become senile, forgetting even the names of their children, or how to eat or walk. I should feel better, but I don't. Or at least I do feel better for a moment or two. But other people's grief doesn't help in the end. It's a long road, and one walks it alone.

It's a relief to be able to talk to you, Dev. We didn't talk enough, not really. It always seemed heavy at the time, but I wish we had. Now I'm chewing your ears off!

&

And it isn't just birth, copulation and death that are different for us, Maya says, but grief too. Bombay is not India, thank goodness, and no one will come along to shave my head or parade Maya through the streets on a donkey. For us it isn't social grief—the cursed widow and the rest of that baloney—but personal, and only we can come to terms with it. Alone. Hard luck.

True. A little frightening, a little exhilarating, but true.

&

Dear Dev,

I think you would be pleased with me. I'm not a wax dummy any more. Sometimes the right shoulder feels real, sometimes the left. Sometimes the heart flies back. I'm almost human. Being human seems to be an ambition that's worth it these days. I read about such horrendous things. There was this programme on Japanese germ warfare scientists in Manchuria who fed starving Chinese children rice cakes with cholera bacteria in them. Tourists and journalists are being kidnapped and beheaded on video. You can't go down the same river twice, but we seem to do that again and again. It's completely outside my comprehension. 'Ordinary', 'decent' suddenly seem to be the highest we can attain. So here's to ordinary people.

I miss you, Dev. *We* miss you. What is it like up there?

ॐ

A long, annoyed e-mail from Deblina: 'I read this article about some new beastie called "arranged love marriages", and Indians settled abroad are going back to India for them, whatever they are. XYZ says he was born and grew up in the States but his heart is in India. What are we supposed to say? Wah! Wah!? Damn hypocrites. You can't go to a country just to make money and then talk about it as if everything and everybody is shit. Somebody could easily write a book here called *The Ugly Indian*. There are so many varieties. Mallu Associates, Tam-Brahm

Associations, Saligao Associations (and we wonder why nobody loves us!). Suddenly one's supposed to have all this fellow feeling for guys one would never mix with at home. Harvard, MIT, designer jeans and a bit of an accent and then 'mummee, daddee'. It's all so superficial. They don't question anything and they think they're modern.

The guy who has written the article is some Dhruv something. He's a big noise with the Asian rag I look at in my masochistic moods. I mean, he just strings together quotes from various people and that's supposed to be journalism. No comment, nothing. I am sending him a fierce e-mail.'

ಐ

Dear Deblina,

Dev used to say you shouldn't be surprised when people are stupid, you should be surprised when they are not! It's a very consoling saying. I used to know a Dhruv something, it could well be the same person. I.G. Deblina. It isn't worth the aggro.

Love,
Sim

∞

Dhruv. A month or so after I became engaged to Dev, I met casually at a neighbour's a 'boy' I thought I'd like to marry. He was down from the States and was on vacation with an American friend, Ron. They were going trekking. He was so sick of relatives and neighbours that he couldn't wait to be off. They teased him about forgetting Indian customs, customs he had never been particularly interested in. 'They keep explaining all these rigmaroles to Ron,' he said. 'I mean, why can't they just chat? Ron's not into sociological curiosities.'

I did not discover what Ron was into as he merely nodded his head. 'And they're such hypocrites,' Dhruv went on, 'they go to the States to make money, and spend their time talking about how immoral whites are.'

I nodded, only half-listening, savouring instead a strange and exciting little current that seemed to burble through my veins.

I had fantasized about him for days, Sim and Dhruv in a passionate clinch. I had never got beyond passionate clinches, partly because I wasn't sure what happened next, partly because Dhruv's constant chatter would interrupt the fantasy. He had certainly thought me a bore as I sat there with a vacuous smile.

During the eighty-third or so round of this fantasy, it occurred to me to wonder if Dev ever had fantasies about anyone else. I was startled by the thought, and worried by it. Before I got to the passionate clinch this time, I said to Dhruv, 'I'm engaged, you see.' Ron, chewing a toothpick, nodded.

Well, Dhruv would certainly find a great deal to complain about India now.

He was far away, married to a girl my mother described as an 'American barmaid'. How she arrived at such a conclusion was hard to say, since she had never seen a barmaid of any kind. But typical. Dhruv was right. Indians are a bore.

As for Dev, he had once laughingly said he had admired a girl in college. She was called 'Golden' because her light brown hair caught the light and shone like a halo. I decided on the spot that I hated Golden. I asked Dev sourly what came of it. 'Nothing,' he had said. 'Dosa-type places weren't her style, so I admired her from afar. She wore her hair loose and tossed it from side to side.'

'And you slavered?'

'I slavered.'

It's odd, but stray lines from some of the books and poems I read in college suddenly surface. I mean, I used to learn bits I liked, and read things, but I didn't like writing critical appreciations or explaining why I liked something. I likes what I likes.

Our teacher, who had probably heard students say this kind of thing a million times would say, 'That's a romantic idea Simran. A poem which has lasted a couple of hundred years will survive your attempts to analyse it.' We were all full of pretty half-baked ideas. We used to quote a verse to annoy her:

Poet: *O cuckoo, shall I call thee bird*
                  Or but a wandering voice?
Examiner: *State the alternative preferred.*
                  Give reasons for your choice.

'You're lazy, Simran,' the teacher said, 'intelligent, but lazy.'

'O the mind, mind has mountains; cliffs of fall.' Spot on. I still have the anthology we used, with my notes scribbled in the margins. I'm catching up now. What a fool I had been, a complacent provincial like I said my mother was.

When Ved rang, and said as always, 'Simi-jaan, what's new?' I told him.

He was nonplussed. 'Poetry,' he said, as if a dog had just peed on his shoe. For once he was at a loss for words.

'Yes Ved, that stuff that rhymes, you know, and sometimes doesn't rhyme.'

'I thought it always had to rhyme, June-moon and shit like that.'

'I'm joking,' I said, to cut short a pointless conversation.

Ved was relieved. 'So tell me then, what's new?'

೮೨

'You're becoming a recluse, Sim,' friends have begun to say. 'Soon you won't leave your room.'

It's not like that. I'm happy to hear from them, see them.

I once saw a painting called 'Silence'. It was painted white all over and had just one yellow spot in a corner. Taped music had filled the gallery, some inept woman moaning out a raga. I didn't know what to make of it. Now I know, and it's nothing to do with blank whiteness.

Weird to recall the way I would stand at the window and look at the birds Dev called me to see. He never got tired of them, especially golden orioles, but I would be impatient because I was in the middle of whisking an egg for an omelette or some such. Seems ridiculous now, to exchange an omelette for an oriole. But perhaps I'm just getting sentimental in retrospect. Omelettes had to be made, after all. No one lives life as if death is around the corner.

৪০

E-mail from Deblina: 'Come West, young woman. Available: divorced men in good condition. I recommend the Eng. Lit. prof. My own hunk has moved on to where all good hunks move on—a blonde hunkee. No matter. Plenty more where he came from.'

E-mailed back: 'Hang on to them while I catch up on the Ten Best Books of the Year.'

Deblina: 'Don't bother to read. You can make megabucks moaning about being exiled from your roots, and being forced to communicate in an alien tongue. And don't do a Dev on me and say it isn't alien. I'm saying it pays to say it is alien. You can write bad poems and say they are multicultural. Then you can whine about not being put on the syllabus. You can talk about Ancient Culture, and never mind the filthy public lavatories.'

৪০

50

It's a relief to natter with Deblina, Vimi and Rishad. They seem to accept me without questions. They do not mark me, on a scale of 1 to 10, on how I'm 'coping'.

ଞ

Ved

I CAN'T BELIEVE IT, I just can't believe it. It's like losing an arm or a leg. We were planning one of our boys'-own weekends at my farm near Sanjana and the next thing we knew was . . . Shit! What a thing to happen.

Dev loved that farm. We'd play Pink Floyd, and zoot, and drive to the beach. Sim once said, 'You guys ought to be married to each other.' But it wasn't like that. I don't know how to explain it, but it's different. No ego hassles when women aren't around. You know what I mean, no family furniture. My father thinks, my mother says, and all that shit. I mean, I love my wife and all that, but sometimes I just like to have the guys around.

When the kid died, Dev spent a lot of time at the farm. Bread and eggs from the local shop, a few veggies from the farm, plenty of booze, I'd drop by once in a while, we'd talk about cricket, business problems, problems with my ex-wife, stocks, everything but the kid. He had a life. We had good times. But the kid was unfinished business.

Shit about the good dying young. The good want to live, same as everyone else. I mean, you look at those guys lining up for free meals near the Mahim dargah. You'd think they'd want to jump into the nearest nullah, but there they are, day after day, patiently waiting their turn. I can't work it out. I can't work a lot of things out. A lot of things.

Dev and I met at a local adda near the college we went to. We'd share a joint. I used to meet a dealer at the local cemetery. He always gave me good stuff, and I'd share it with Dev. We still share a joint. I mean, we did.

We were no big-time party guys but we had a good time. More or less interesting jobs, a bit of spare money, plenty of time to hang loose, what else does anyone want?

Dev kept telling me not to marry again. I'd had enough hassles the first time. But cooking for yourself is a pain, man, and I wanted to cuddle at night. Not sex all the time or anything, but a cuddle, like having a giant hot-water bottle around! My wife doesn't like that comparison, but I say, 'Joking, man. Just joking.' I wouldn't have had to explain to Dev. Or to Sohrab, or Amit, or Dilip. We've known each other twenty years, and that makes a difference. Luckily, the girls we've married understand, most of the time that is. They go their way, we go ours. Living in each other's pockets is absolutely out.

I talk to Sim on the phone for an hour sometimes. She needs to get out more often. Most of her friends think so. Even that Maya. I don't understand how Dev and Sim could be friends with this Maya babe. She's full of this feminism trip. I mean, is Sim oppressed? Is my wife oppressed? Is this Maya babe oppressed? If she isn't, I think she should be! Going on about the feelings and the understanding shit. And now the pansies are getting into this act! A little flick of the wrist and a wriggle, and 'I'm oppressed', 'Society doesn't understand us'. 'Are you straight?' one of these wimps said to me once. I thought he was talking about my business dealing! I said yeah, man, I treat all my workers well, I pay off the local goons, what more do you want? He giggled! Whenever I see him at the club I go the other way. Fuck, man, what a menagerie!

My wife and I have had Sim over since Dev's death. We keep it easy. We go for a drive, have a drink, chat the chat. I know what she feels. She knows what I feel. No need to make a drama out of it. That's life, man. 'Ved,' Sim said yesterday, 'I'm glad you're around.'

The orange-red leaves of the almond tree are falling. There's a nip in the air. Heavy symbolism, what?

∞

'Maya,' I said, 'it's been three months. I just can't believe it. Time passes. Life passes. Been feeling a bit of a widower myself. Don't get me wrong. But Dev and I talked almost every day, and he told me his plans, and I told him mine. Women can really eat a man's head, don't you think? Or don't you think?'

'Don't be silly, Ved,' Maya said, irritated. 'It's not as if I think women can do no wrong.'

'Cool it babe, just a joke.'

'Oh well.'

'Seen Sim recently? She seems to spend a lot of time with those kids. They were there the last time I dropped in. I don't think they took a shine to me.'

'I suppose they don't keep telling her what to do with her life.'

'Is anyone telling her what to do with her life?'

'She seems to think so.'

'You're sounding frosty, babe. Sim giving you the cold shoulder?'

'Don't be silly. It's just that I'm in the middle of something.'

'Why didn't you say?'

'You didn't ask.'

'Okay. Stay in touch.'

This Maya bimbette, she gets my goat. Earnest as hell. It confused Maya that Dev and Sim had somehow made a go of things. Well, they did and they didn't, and that goes for most people. Maya doesn't understand that. She says, what's the point? Why bother with the inconvenience of having someone under your feet all the time, smoking out the place, demanding three meals a day, if it isn't some kind of absolute thing. The point is, Maya honey, that's the way things are. Most marriages are marriages of convenience with some affection thrown in and all that. Habit, most marriages are a habit, and habits are hard to break. Dev once said to Maya, 'It doesn't do to go around with your tongue hanging out.' Damn crude. Maya was hurt, but Dev was suddenly bugged by something she said, as we all are from time to time. 'Sim loves me in her own way,' Dev said to Maya one day, and after that she was a little wary of him.

What Maya doesn't admit ever is that Sim doesn't trust her. Not entirely, that is. Maya tends or tended to repeat things she had been told and create a kerfuffle. When Dev told her that X wanted to sleep with her only as time pass, that he had no interest in commitment, she promptly told X, and there was a bit of strain between Dev and X after that. Not pleasant, as X was a friend of Dev's. Then, Maya was irritated that Y smoked in private but not in public. She made a point of referring to Y's habit at a party at Dev and Sim's.

I mean, who wants the truth shoved in your face all the time? So you drink whisky in stainless steel glasses and pretend it's holy water. So you pay the linesman a hundred bucks to let you talk on someone else's line for unlimited time abroad. It happens. If I told my wife the things I think about she'd be going back to Mummy.

∽

Ever since Dev died I've been hearing a lot about this gentleness business. I mean, can't a guy tell his mother to fuck off, get off his back? He can, but then there will be all this blackmail. Pappu, come home. Father Serious, mother delirious, sister threatening to jump out of window. And Pappu comes back with his tail between his legs.

Enough. You get the point. Gentleness has its flip side. Weakness. But it would help if, every time Mummy calls out to Pappu when Pappu wants to talk to his wife (Mummy's timing is unerring), he says,

'Look Mother, I want to talk to Pammie.' Mummies, like dogs, recognize fear, and go for the jugular. If Mummy says you can't go away for the weekend because she isn't feeling too good and she may need a doctor, Pappu can refer to his sister who spends her time faffing about anyway. But he doesn't, and life is a bitch for Pammie, who ends up wanting to murder both Pappu and Mummy and everyone else in sight.

Thus, Dev. Not quite Pappu material, but not strong either. He could have been tougher with Simran and told her not to get so hyper every time his mother appeared. It was, after all, just a matter of a day or two. He could have told Mummy to wipe that long-suffering look off her face, even if he wouldn't quite use those words. He could have told his boys' club that it would be pleasant to have the wives along once in a way. He could have stuck around when the kid died. It was tough on Sim, but I didn't want to interfere. I rang Sim from time to time but just got these zombie sort of replies.

My wife and I gave little Sara a huge teddy bear. It disappeared with Sara. If she had grown up she would have been a beauty.

☙

I suppose I could meet Sim more often, take her out. But there's the wife.

'Let's ask Sim to have Sunday breakfast with us at that Maharashtrian joint in Dadar.'

'You can ask her if you want to. I'm not coming.'

'What kind of shit is that?'

'I know your kind. Putting a fatherly arm around her.'

'She's my friend's wife.'

'All your friends have wives.'

'So what are you saying?'

'Nothing. You're a very fatherly man.'

'Don't be sarcy. What's eating you?'

'Nothing.'

'So bugger off.'

'Don't talk to me like that.'

'How do you want me to talk to you?'

'All this Simi-jaan stuff.'

'It doesn't mean anything.'

'That's what you say.'

'Shit.'

'I'd like to scratch her eyes out.'

'So go scratch them out.'

Vimi

RISHAD AND I are an item. Rishad, Sim and I are an item. Not 'item' item, so don't get weird ideas.

Rishad likes Sim and feels he must look after her. Rishad likes his dad and feels he must look after him. His mum has gone off to the States to live with Rishad's older sister. I suspect it's a split, but Rishad isn't saying. And Rishad feels he's got to look after me, don't ask me why. The old male thing, I suppose. I worry that he's going to end up hating all of us.

I mean, my mum was like that. Is like that actually. She'd race to Colaba to see how her parents were, then go to her job, then to Santa Cruz to see an old aunt. The aunt had mentioned that she wanted to give my mum her furniture and jewellery, and then told my mum she came to see her only for what she was hoping to get! Silly cow. Mum feels guilty if she doesn't go everywhere and look after everyone. I tell her her generation is a bit mad. She says that's the way she was brought up, but I don't see other women dashing from one end of Bombay to the other.

I can look after myself, thank you. I can't tell Rishad that, but he is amazing. When my previous guy went off in a rage one day, Rishad said, 'Don't go after him, give him five or six months to get over it, not a day less.' I'd ring Rishad and say 'I can't stand it', but he'd just say 'Five months'. And believe it or not the swine turned up after five months, smiling like the sun had come out of his arse.

I can't even tell Rishad that Sim can look after herself. Everyone can, pretty much, without a hundred violins playing 'She loved soft toys. Though she discovered the hard way that life isn't soft. She loved chocolates. Now, she knows life isn't a bitter chocolate. She loved to dream. Does she dream anymore?' Gooey goo, courtesy TOI. And if they think wasting themselves is some bright thing, there isn't a thing you can do about it. Losers are losers, you might as well leave them alone.

Look at that Ma Something-or-the-other in the Sunday supplement, smiling as she kisses an old woman, smiling at a glum patient in a hospital, smiling as she's followed by disciples Indian and phoren, all looking like cretins with their shaven heads. Gives me a depression, does old Ma Sunshine. Old Miss Lobo at school was like that. 'God sends us trials,' she always said, 'but we must at least wake up and say "Thank you God for another day".' Miss Lobo was a trial alright. She was always dashing off to some youth meeting or parish get-together on her brum-brum. She had this word she liked:

Animators. She was an animator. She thought we should all be animators. One look at her and you'd want to be dead again.

Actually, Sim's alright. She doesn't preach or probe. Dev was alright too. I saw Sim with a guy a couple of times. I don't know if she was getting some on the side. Rishad will kill me if I say so. I tell Rishad he's the last of the romantics. He just grins. He's alright, really, I just wish he'd ease up on the daddy-o bit. I'm not much of a mummy-o. I mean, what would I do with a kid? My kid brother drives me crazy. It's like having a typhoon in the house.

The girls in college think Rish is Galahad or whoever. He's sweet, really he is, don't know why I'm griping. He gives me lots of space, doesn't hit the roof everytime I talk to a guy. He's normal enough when we go to a disco or a pub. So what's with? PMT, I suppose. Definitely not my sour nature!

I'm really a bitch! I'm making Rish sound like some pious creep. He isn't that. He's good and naturally that makes me envious. I remember a time when I told him something I hadn't told anyone before. I was so jealous of a baby my mother was fussing over, some cousin's baby son, that I got hold of the flit pump my mother used to kill cockroaches. I thought the flit would work on the baby. I was four at the time. Luckily my mother came in while I was struggling with the pump. The bloody thing was nearly as big as I was. It didn't help the baby's cause that my mother took a chappal and beat my bottom blue. I thought Rish would have a fit. He didn't, he hugged me and said 'I love you, Vims.' How do you deal with that?

And a dead baby—how do you deal with that? Now with Dev gone, how does Sim cope?

ജ

Maya

DEAR DEBS,

Guess what. Peter has been transferred back to London and will leave in three months. He has told me, with unusual firmness, to make up my tiny mind and come with him. I don't know what to do. I get flabby in a relationship and too attached and my world revolves around that person. I can't stand the idea of that happening again. Peter says flex them (my emotional muscles!) for a few months and then turn up, minus cartons of basmati rice and dal. But when I think seriously about leaving this place, I feel like a rat deserting a sinking ship. I know. I know. If all the rats are doing likewise I'd be mad not to. I told Sim to come along, I'd show her the sights. She says she'll think about it. I don't know what there is to think about. She does nothing here, she can do nothing there.

Help me to make up my tiny mind.

☙

'Maybe she needs time alone,' Peter said when I complained about not seeing much of Sim.

'But it's been six months now.'

'That's not a very long time, Maya, to grieve, I mean. She was rushed off her feet the first few months.'

'I don't know. She's gone a bit weird. The other day she said she was coming over with some Smirnoff and soda and lemons and would I see there was enough ice. I forgot, and there wasn't. And she started that mouth-in-thin-line and eyes-glittering stuff she used to use on her mother-in-law, and hardly spoke. I was quite annoyed.'

'I'd be annoyed if there wasn't enough ice,' Peter said with an annoying smile.

'Everything's a joke for you. You're damn irritating Peter,' I said. I could feel a quarrel twirling its way into my head. 'And for god's sake don't say I'm in a naughty temper. I'll kill you.'

'So I'm irritating. So I'm not a saint. I don't want you to be a saint either. That would be very trying. Just ease up, won't you?'

'So sensible,' I said meanly.

'You make it sound gruesome.'

'It is gruesome.'

'Okay. So I won't offer you lunch at the new Thai place.'

'Don't offer.'

Debs, where are you? I didn't get an answer to my last e-mail, the angst-ridden one. Can you stand some more, not really angst angst this time but thereabouts? I don't think Ved likes me. In fact I'm sure he doesn't. I tried to tell Peter about it but he said since I didn't like him either what were the odds. I lost my shirt again. When I told Peter that I thought Ved had the hots for Sim, he said he wasn't surprised. That started me off again. You can imagine how it went. Peter said he imagined a lot of guys had the hots for Sim, she seemed so distant and unavailable. So I said I suppose I'm horribly obvious and he said no, you're upfront. And I said I suppose that's boring, so why don't you go and fuck Sim, so he said . . . you know, the usual reasonable bastard stuff:

'What's got into you?'

'You haven't answered my question. Are you bored with me or something?'

'Maya, don't be daft.'

'You're not answering my question.'

'If I were bored with you every time I found a woman attractive I would have been a long way away by now.'

'Maybe you wish you were.'

'Maya, I really don't want to go on with this discussion. It's absurd.'

'You're just evading the issue.'

'Okay, so I'm evading the issue.'

'I feel like slapping Sim.'

I don't know what the matter is with me, Debs. Do you?

ക

'Complications,' Peter said one day.

'Oh?'

'My wife's found another, and the kids aren't happy, especially because the other has kids as well.'

I didn't know what to say. Was Peter trying to tell me that I'd be yet another complication? I decided to ask straight out. He sort of hesitated. I mean, I said, what with me being Indian and all that.

'I don't know,' Peter said. 'I mean, it may be a problem, but they could handle it. I just feel they have a lot on their plate just now.'

'So you don't want me to come to England?'

'I do. But I need to think it out. I've only just heard. I'd like to spend some time with them in England before I introduce anything new to them.'

'I'm the something new?'

'Don't be touchy, Maya. You know what I mean.'

'I'm not being touchy,' I said, though I was. 'I've got to think about it as well.'

'So good. We'll both think.'

'Sensible as always.'

'Don't bitch, Maya.'

'See you,' I said and stalked off, working out already what I would say to Sim and Debs.

ജ

'I only know that he who forms a tie is lost. The germ of corruption has entered his soul.' The epigraph from my favourite Greene novel.

I am beginning to be convinced I have no talent for relationships. All these ups and downs; I feel drained by them. The snag is, he who doesn't form a tie is also lost. Somehow causes are no substitute. And I used to preach to Sim because I thought she had compromised by sticking it out with Dev even when they went through a bad patch. She hadn't been really happy, but perhaps she wanted security rather than happiness, and, in any case, Dev had become a habit. A pleasant enough habit, but Sim missed out. Not the Mills and Boon stuff, but a more obvious kind of cherishing.

But Dev was Dev, and someone else may not have turned out to be a better bet at all. I can't imagine Sim with anyone else.

Perhaps 'corruption' is too strong a word, then. It's life. One can't be too absolute about anything. Look where absoluteness has brought so many of us. It is absolutes that corrupt.

I must tell Sim I had been wrong to hassle her.

೮೦

Perhaps I'm caught in a trap of automatic gestures, like those irritating images that are always on TV: news about Muslims invariably accompanied by the sound of the muezzin and skull-capped heads bowing in prayer, Africans dancing and singing, and orthodox Jews bobbing in front of that wall. The whole caboodle. Why should I think that because my father walked out everyone would walk out on me, Peter included? Why can't I remember the more pleasant interactions with my mother—the way we had laughed together at the kind of swimsuit that she and the other members of the swimming pool thought fit to wear? My mother had had to learn swimming when she was over fifty, to exercise her joints, and there she was in a swimsuit that reached down to her knees, with long sleeves, a skirt over it, and a blouse on top! Then there were those lessons I helped mother prepare when a neighbour wanted to learn English. The neighbour didn't pay of course, just brought her a quarter kilo of some rather dry pedas from Rajkot.

৪৩

Dear Debs,

A few phone calls from Peter and then a letter. I feared the worst when I saw the letter. I thought it's something Peter can't say to me in case I shriek over the phone. Well, the kids are with Peter while the wife's new husband and their children settle in. Apparently the younger of Peter's two kids has only just worked out that the new guy is not there for her entertainment and resents it. Peter says he takes them out but they trail along listlessly to parks, zoos, toy departments. He says he feels like an incompetent DIY man trying to patch up things that are falling apart.

They're not going to be with Peter for always. They'll sort of divide their time. It all sounds rather messy. I certainly don't know how to help. You know how I am about children. And it's difficult. I've got enough baggage of my own. Oh well. Bumble on regardless.

Ved rang but I was in no mood to talk to him. I said I'd ring back. And then I got this very weird call from a guy I vaguely knew years ago. He's not someone I keep in touch with, or want to. He said my name and then stopped as if he expected me to recognize his voice and shriek for joy. He said he wanted to bring me up to date on what he had been doing, and insisted I take down his number and address. He said he was now living on his own and asked when I would drop in. I'm surprised he didn't say he wanted to show me his etchings.

And don't write back and say 'Ha ha ha and ha'; I'll kill you.

∞

At last an e-mail from Debs: 'Sorry, Maya, I had an assignment deadline, and the prof. is not the kind you can bat your eyes at and wriggle a bit. You're really in a state, aren't you? Forget about Ved, he's of no importance. I don't know what to say about Peter. He seems a little bland to me, but maybe that's just the reserved English bit. Maybe he has strange dark yearnings under all that, like that actor fellow Hugh whatever. You expect too much from guys, Maya. Look at the guys we know. I prefer my women friends, even dear Sim who does nothing at all. Guys are handy when you get the itch, but I worry about anything long term. I mean, suppose I outgrow them? And it's so boring to keep starting again and going through the same routine. Of course here the routine is pretty quick—hamburgers and rumble-tumble. Not that I've tumbled so far. Try it out, say to yourself you'll go to England for a year or two and see how you feel. Play it 'by the ear' as they say in good old Bombay.

I'm sorry. I don't seem to be able to think of anything really helpful to say. I know you feel 'home is where you have to gather grace' and all that, but my feeling is you can gather grace pretty much anywhere. A handy characteristic, but not one to endear you to the rootswallahs. F— the rootswallahs is what I say, and f— Ved. Rootswallahs carry their homes with them; you should see the lot here. I just refused an invitation for Diwali shenanigans. I mean, what the hell.'

Dear Debs,

Such wisdom in one so young! Where do you guys learn it and how? Yes, that is the point, or one of them anyway—I'm afraid I'll outgrow these guys or they'll outgrow me. All these ads for people who want to marry. I don't know how they have the nerve. Maybe they don't think about it. Maybe it's the done thing and they do it. I remember one of our elderly neighbours telling me how one of her daughters was harassed by the in-laws and how unhappy she was, and in the next breath telling me of her plans to marry off the second daughter.

The situation with Peter is tricky just now with the children sulking and so forth, and I don't want to add to the pressure by moaning to him about what's happening in my tiny mind.

I'm bored by the research I'm doing. It seems pretty futile. In any case no one gives a damn about research. They think it's a money-wasting, time-wasting bourgeois activity. They feel we ought to be out organizing protests and doing street plays. I mean, crowds will collect for just about anything as long as they can gape. One or two of these activists had only working-class men and women at their wedding and sang working-class songs, whatever they are.

Revolution, revolution, revolution, no doubt. I want
lots of white wine at my wedding, and I shall lie
under a table and sing Anglo-Saxon ballads. And maybe
I'll meet Jeremy Irons one day and he'll be free and
willing!

Love,
Maya

୫

'Do you know what Mrs Dey said to me not long
ago?' Peter said.
    'Do tell.'
    'She said an Indian girl would do anything to marry
an Englishman.'
    'She's done a fair bit of marrying herself. Five, or
is it six, husbands? I don't know how she has the
energy. Wasn't one German?'
    'Yes. He was looking for a peaceful Asian wife, not
a raucous European one.'
    'I should have taken him to Churchgate at rush
hour to watch peaceful Asian women stampeding.
Anyway, what did you say? You agreed with her?'
    'Naturally.'
    'Scumbag.'

'Have you made up your tiny mind or not?'

'How can I after what Mrs Dey said?'

'Fuck Mrs Dey.'

'I don't want to. Har har.'

'I think I shall have to be firm with you,' Peter said. 'I'm going to give you a deadline.'

༄

Simran is reading a book on rebirth or reincarnation or whatever that someone has lent her. A psychiatrist and his patient remember her previous births together. At first he is sceptical but then he believes.

Simran is horrified, not because the psychiatrist ends up believing, but because of what the patient reveals. Apparently she has been through hundreds of rebirths, and in each she has exactly the same mother, the same father, the same husband, the same friends.

'You mean, you don't want me around again?'

'No,' Simran says, 'I want to meet new people if I have to go through all that.'

I point two fingers at her in a shooting sign. Simran says, 'But really, wouldn't you like to meet new people?'

'Maybe.'

'If I can't I'd really have no rebirths at all. This book has really given me the heebie-jeebies.'

'Forget it,' I say. 'Come and help me with this-world problems.'

&

Rishad

MY MOTHER SAYS she's losing her memory, she can't remember names. Then she goes through the alphabet and stops at 'S' and looks at me over her glasses. So I remind her about the ancient uncle who tried to push her into a corner and kiss her. She laughs and says 'All in a day's work' and I tell her that sounds pretty dubious, people would misunderstand. That's what people are for, she says, to misunderstand. She's pretty cool, my mum, though she's over fifty. At least she's realized she has to stop saying 'Recite a poem for the aunties' at her bridge club. I mean, I'll be twenty next month.

'You're sweet,' she says sometimes, 'not one of those *ineffective* guys.' I don't know what she means. My father isn't exactly ineffective, he's a CEO. Vimi says I'm sweet too, but she says it in a sour way. 'What's with this sweet business?' I said to her. 'It's not as if I do anything I don't want to.' She says the things I *want* to do are sweet. I give up. I know she's a bit mad because of the time I spend, we spend, with Sim.

Sim showed me Dev's school reports yesterday. Lots of red lines and smarmy remarks: 'Could do better in Maths, Science, History, Geography and Languages.'

I asked her why he had kept them. 'I don't know,' Sim said. 'They were there among his papers. Perhaps they amused him.'

'Mixed a good cocktail,' I said, 'could remember cricket scores from the year dot, could cook if he wanted to, and etc. He once called himself an armchair unintellectual.'

'All of that,' Sim said. 'And full of nuggets of useless information about cars, bikes, gizmos of every kind which he and Ved exchanged with the greatest zest. I don't know what to do with half the stuff he bought, dust-busters, lemon squeezers, special pads for cleaning the leaves of house plants.'

'My mother'll take the lemon squeezer. It'll look fancy at her parties. And the dust-buster as a conversation piece. That'll get them off the gossip for a bit, and running down each other's bridge scores.'

'Take the lot,' Sim said.

Mum, Dad and I had taken Sim to the club the other evening, and this bozo with badly-dyed hair all unevenly coloured came up to say something to Dad. We introduced him to Sim and he immediately asked for her phone number! Mum nearly choked on her drink. This is supposed to be a classy club, and it's full of all these guys with paunches and shrunk shanks. And the women are all loud and covered in gold. Dad was all apologetic so I said, 'Cool it dad, a creep's a creep.'

৪৩

I can't wait to start working and living on my own. Simbly. Not because living at home's a pain or anything. What I'd really love is one of those old houses in those villagey areas in the city. Vimi says they're not going to last much longer, and I wouldn't want a builder's goons to come after me. Vimi is sad because the Bombay she loves is disappearing, and we're getting these glass monstrosities instead.

My dad's giving me a car for my birthday. I told Vimi I'll take her for the first ride, and we'll sit on the beach, and eat bhel, and that kind of stuff. Big deal, she said. Vim's okay, really. She just likes being sour. She likes my mum. They bad-mouth me together.

Vimi once gave me this toad thing, you know, the kind with a message saying, 'You've got to kiss a lot of toads before you meet the handsome prince.' I must show it to Sim. Anyway, nice to know I'm the handsome prince!

೮೩

Simran

DEV HAD BEEN to England for a few months before we married, visiting one of his adda friends from his college days. 'Pub-crawling,' Dev had said when I asked him what they had done with their time. I don't know what I'll do if I go there. The parks, maybe, and Kew Gardens. Maya will drag me to poetry readings.

Maya had spent a year or two in England, doing odd jobs, moving from a brief stint wiping counters and making coffee in a sari shop to working with a lefty lawyer on minority cases, editing a minority newsletter. It put her off minorities, she said. There was that dancer who had gone for a festival and was horrified that people used only toilet paper and no water. Dance was sacred, she had said, and she found it difficult to dance thinking of all those unwashed arses in the audience.

Everyone asks Maya why she came back to India. She isn't sure herself, especially after she found the relatives she was staying with for a while rummaging in her suitcase and reading her diary. She hoped to be useful, she said, make some difference, be a big fish in little waters. I think she regrets her idealism. She keeps saying the city is a cesspit, outside of a

92

few spots that have been 'beautified'. She's told Deblina never to think of coming back, it just isn't worth it.

Why does she stay? 'Familiarity,' she says. 'It's a familiar cesspit.'

ⁿ

I don't really want to go to England, or the US, at least not just now. Nothing cosmic, just the sight of barbets in the trees (the golden orioles have left, winter is over), Rishad and Vimi popping in, the smell of jasmine from the balcony below. And the call of the muezzin in the early dawn. The man has a slightly quavering, melancholy voice. The melancholy seeps into one's bones and makes the world real in a way that page three romps never do.

I'm not ready yet to be jolted by new landscapes, new sounds, new people. Maya would understand. Deblina would be furious with what she would call my stupidity. Ved would be puzzled and say, 'Simi-jaan, what's all this thinking-phinking shit?'

ⁿ

Dear Dev,

I don't know what the matter is with all of us. I rang
Maya to tell her about this stray dog I've made friends
with. I call him Dog with Attitude. And she just
snapped and said she knew a pig with attitude. I
don't know if she meant me. Then Ved rang and
started all this Simi-jaan stuff and I snapped at him
and said what's all this Simi-jaan nonsense. So *he*
retired offended. Maybe it's the heat.

I told Rishad about the dog. He sits on top of a
garbage heap at the bottom of the road (the dog
does!), looking with disdain at the world. For the
last few days I've been taking him biscuits and he
looks at me as if I'm mad. I end up eating a lot of
biscuits I don't want! Rishad said not to let him get
me down. It took him a year to make friends with
his own dog.

There's another fat slob who howls with delight,
knowing I've brought a snack for him, and there's a
pup who comes rushing the moment he sees me,
jumps on my lap and rests his head against my
shoulder. Nice. And then yesterday the Dog with
Attitude descended from his garbage heap, walked
up to me, wagged his tail and turned on his tum.

Surrender! I'm thrilled with my conquest. I shall buy him a great, fat, slobbery gulab jamun.

৪৩

I told Rishad about my conquest of the Dog with Attitude.

'Brilliant!' Rishad said. 'He doesn't trust too many people.'

'So I'm thrilled.'

Rishad smiled.

'I feel I've been living like a zombie,' I said. 'Maybe I am a zombie.'

'Zombies don't usually know they are zombies, or don't admit they are.'

'You're a comfort, Rishad, did I ever tell you that?'

'Come to think of it, you haven't.'

'So I'm telling you now. I don't know how I would have managed without you all these months.'

'I think I'll roll over and show you my tum.'

The young are remarkable. They are involved in and knowledgeable about so many things, they are clear about what they want to do, they have their own cars and mobiles. Vimi strides around unselfconsciously in short shorts. It doesn't even occur to her that she should be self-conscious. What a bhondu I had been at their age. I would have been too nervous even to hold hands with a boy.

&

'How are you Simi-jaan? Long time no hear.'

'How are you, Ved?'

'What can I say? Can't live with, can't live without.'

'A mysterious utterance. What does it mean?'

'Marriage.'

'What's brought that on?'

'Same old thing, yaar. Possessive shit.'

'What have you been up to?'

'Nothing. Wifey says I have the hots for you.'

'Oh. Tell her I'll give you a character certificate.'

'No! She'll know I've been talking to you.'

'As bad as that?'

'As bad as that. You were lucky. Dev and you went your own ways.'

'Yes, but they were straight ways, you old lech.'

'What are you saying, yaar? Me a lech! A thousand times no.'

'A thousand times yes.'

'What about that Rishad guy? He have the hots for you?'

'Don't you ever think about anything but hots?'

'Sometimes. Food. Drink. Zoot.'
'Try poetry.'
'Shit.'

ॐ

What had Dev seen in Ved? Perhaps guys are less judgemental in their friendships. Not that Dev hadn't complained about how stingy Ved could be, or how little he contributed to their trips.

Outside the ICU Ved had said, 'Tell Dev "Cheers! And one for the road"' and I, like a fool, repeated it unthinkingly. I could have kicked myself. Still, maybe Dev would have been amused if it registered. I don't know how much registered, he was so there and not there all the time.

He knew he was dying. But he seemed to take it so lightly. He said, 'You know Sim, the little buggers are taking revenge.' I said, 'What little buggers?' In his final school exam, he said, he couldn't remember the word 'corpuscles' no matter how hard he tried. So, throughout the essay on the circulation of blood he had written 'those little red things in the blood'.

ॐ

The flip side of Silent Suffering Smile seems to be manipulation.

Dev's mother was going through a particular conversation for the third time.

'Are you sure you want to give me all these sheets and bedspreads?' said ma-in-law.

'Yes, I'm sure.'

'But they must have cost a lot. Maybe you should keep them for guests.'

'I've thought about it. I want you to have them.'

'That's sweet of you. But if you change your mind or want them back, you have only to say so.'

'I won't change my mind.'

'All right then. But I really think . . .'

And so on, till I wondered whether to kill her now or later.

'We've been through this conversation several times.'

'Oh, don't be offended. I was only thinking . . .'

I turned and walked away.

All this kerfuffle about sheets. I mean, does she have to turn old saris into sheets, curtains, quilts, cushions, with nothing quite matching? It's not as if she can't afford new things.

Maya says I'm a bit unfair, she did after all move into her own flat when Dev and I got married. Yeah, well, she probably had a bad time as a young wife and all that. I don't really want to know. Maya is really too preachy sometimes.

I felt bad later. I shouldn't increase the tension, if only because old so-and-so would have more reason to whine. No, I shouldn't increase the tension because I'm left feeling lousy. Nothing happens to the old girl. Anyway, I spent enough time creating tension when Dev was around.

Some people can't change (or is it that the old girl won't?). So the people who *can* change have to do all the work.

Highfunda—the phrase Rishad would have used. Maybe, the old girl just does not know how to take. Some people just don't. They might give you things readily enough, but are not exactly gracious about receiving. They squirm till they have given you something of approximately the same worth.

Perhaps I should give the old girl a call and apologize. No. That is going too far. I'd play it by ear and try to avoid a fuss the next time round. Or take the things back, and call the old girl's bluff. That would teach her!

Stop it Sim. You're not two years old.

A funny business, kindness. You can be kind but not considerate. I remember the time mother and I had visited some friends in the north. The friends had not allowed us to pay for a thing, not even for the gifts we wanted to bring back for relatives. They were kind, but rather overwhelming. It had cramped our style. We had stopped shopping, and Delhi was the place for shopping.

ഇ

Dear Dev,

And so I'm left with your mother and her Patient Smile. One of life's little ironies. No Dev. No Sara. Only a woman I can barely stand.

It worries me that I can barely remember Sara's face. I remember grey eyes and a fuzzy pink bundle. I don't even know what was done with her ashes. And I couldn't ask you. Weeks away at that farm and then you came back and didn't say a word about anything. Perhaps that was your way of coping. What, after all, was there to say? As always. I don't want to think about it. I feel a kind of rage when I do.

Maya was right. There were too many things we didn't talk about. But is Maya's the better way, upfront about every emotion? I don't suppose it's a question of better or worse, but what we can do and can't do.

I don't want to feel rage. I really don't. Sara's death made me feel punch-drunk, both eyes bleeding. I couldn't talk about it. Somehow the melodrama of grief is almost more upsetting than the event itself: the eyes filling up, the suddenly assumed concerned look, perhaps even the relief that the persons we were grieving for were still safe, what had happened had happened to someone else.

Really, everything's senseless.

ॐ

Dear Dev,

I've just given up on a really stupid book. In every story the man is a brute. In every story the woman is doing something 'wildly', 'desperately'. The author is well known but doesn't understand simple things. It's the silences and sulks, the evasions, the weakness that passes for good nature—that's what wears one down.

I feel the rage coming on again. Perhaps it's better than feeling blank, but it's not an emotion I enjoy. Maybe I should go up on the terrace and scream when no one's about. Or join one of those Laughter Clubs which drive the neighbourhood crazy. Anything is easier than saying I could have killed you sometimes. I am going to tear up this letter. This book has got under my skin. I feel battered by all those adverbs.

∞

'Are you wildly, desperately thinking about your sorrows?' I asked Maya the next day.

'No,' she said, 'should I?'

'Apparently all women do.'

'I'm not all women.'

'Thank goodness for that.'

'Anyway, what's this wildly, desperately lark?'

'Some nonsense I'm reading.'

'What I'm doing is making a list of presents.'

'Presents? Don't tell me you've decided to leave with Peter?'

'Naah. Presents for my friends which Peter will take.'

'Need any help?'

'With the shopping. Then we can "do" lunch.'

'Fine. In an hour's time?'

'In an hour's time.'

∞

I decided to have a farewell party for Peter and rang a few friends. Ved, for one.

'You're inviting me to a party for Peter?' Ved said. 'What about Mrs Peter?'

'No Mrs Peter. Maya isn't going yet.'

'Discreet Sim! He's ditched her.'

'He hasn't ditched her. She just isn't going now. He is.'

'Okay, have it your way. Just as well she isn't going. She would have the subcontinent visiting her in London.'

'That bad, is it?'

'Worse. My wife's elder sister lives in London. Even people who barely know her want her address. Ancient Indian Pile-on.'

'Luckily Peter lives outside London.'

'Simi-jaan, they would have expected Maya to drive them in. If my wife's sister says no to anybody there's hell to pay. Someone did someone a favour, so sister-in-law has to help return the favour.'

'No different from being here.'

'Exactly. I hope you're not thinking of going phoren.'

'Not at the moment anyway.'

'I'll have no one to tell my troubles to,' Ved said.

'You're not going to tell me your wife doesn't understand you.'

'She doesn't understand me. She follows me around with ashtrays. Some shitty Shyam Ahuja rugs, so hell to pay.'

'Difficult.'

'Me or my wife?'

'Shyam Ahuja rugs. Unless you live in air-conditioned splendour.'

'Tell her that, yaar. She says I'm a slob.'

ೞ

The party for Peter was not a success. He was sweet and brought me flowers and champagne, but there was too much tension in the air. Maya not easy with Peter, Ved not easy with Maya, Rishad a bit bewildered, Vimi smiling sourly at all of them, and my mother-in-law dropping in by chance and saying, 'Oh, a party. I'm so sorry. I wouldn't have come over if I had known,' and everyone trying to make her feel at ease, and me wishing she would vamoose and not do her usual routine.

'That must be a record for apologies,' Ved said after she finally left.

Ved's wife said, 'Behave yourself. It's Sim's mother-in-law.'

'Sim doesn't like her, do you Sim?' he said.

Rishad broke in and said, 'So what are you going to do in London, Peter?' even though he knew, and that stupid Ved who had had one champagne too many said, 'Arre bachcha, why you are trying to keep the peace? Everyone is fine.' And Vimi said to Ved, 'Listen, you arsehole, dry up.' And then Ved's wife said . . .

Ye gods! Then Ved got senty and said, 'We really miss Dev,' and I found myself with tears in my eyes, not with grief but at the debacle. Rishad gave me a hug when he was leaving. 'It'll pass,' he said sagely. I didn't even smile.

Most of the food was left untouched. I ate chicken curry for the next two days and then decided to give the dogs a treat.

I asked Maya the next day whether Peter had said anything. 'Why should he?' she said. I said because it was pretty damn awful.

'You know,' Maya said, 'I was once with Peter in a neighbouring city that shall remain nameless. We were having dinner, and around us everyone burped and farted like thunder, even lifting their thighs for better effect. Peter, the good Englishman, just went on talking to me about his visit to Japan. I don't know what was more embarrassing, Peter's silence about the whole thing or the fireworks display.'

'So my little disaster was small beer by comparison?'

'Well, you know how it is. Everyone knows and Peter knows we Indians are nature's own. We turn up when we want to turn up, we quarrel when we want to quarrel, we stare when we want to stare, we get smashed and make a scene when we want to get smashed and make a scene . . .'

'That sounds horribly patronizing. Did Peter say that?'

'Peter is never patronizing,' Maya said with some asperity. 'I'm saying that. That's the way we are. What to do?'

'I'll apologize to him.'

'Don't be silly. I.G. Sim. It happens.'

∞

Deblina the lout laughs when I tell her. Her e-mail reads 'Ha ha ha and ha again. I wish I'd been there.' She thinks we all need a break from each other, we've been milling around in the same pond too long. She's probably right. She has some very good friends who live on an island in a New Jersey lake. Wild geese come up to their backyard, and there's canoeing and the odd bit of canoodling. Tempting. Rishad says he'll look after the Dog with Attitude. And Vimi knows a cut-price travel agent. So what am I waiting for?

When I tell Deblina I'm thinking about going as well, she is ecstatic. Bring Maya, she says. She is lining them up for me and for Maya too if she feels like a fling, a final fling. Maya is furious. 'What does she think,' she says, 'that I'm some frustrated maiden aunt?'

'An "elderly girl" as my provincial little town paper used to say, or a "senior maiden",' I say to Maya. That does not improve her mood. And then she laughs. 'I certainly feel,' she says, 'as if I'm not just over the hill but across the whole bloody range.'

ॐ

Deblina

I WONDER IF Maya really wants to marry anybody. I wonder if she knows what she wants at all. I mean, she keeps getting involved with these non-starter guys, married, divorced and intending to keep it that way, guys with weird problems. There was this guy, some lecturer in philosophy who didn't like to take off his undoos, and when he finally did, he ran away, just about stopping to put on his trousers. He couldn't get it up, I suspect. He was amusing to talk to, Maya said. Amusing is Maya's thing. She said he apologized years later. He was very immature she said, and was on some spiritual crap and felt he had—what was that phrase Mother Superior used—'fallen from grace'. Charming. She even fancied Dev at one stage. Poor Dev. For all his cool I suspect he must have ducked under his quilt and stayed there till she got over it.

But Sim knows what she wants. She's always known, for all that floating about like she's some leaf in the wind. Do people have to *do* something to be worthwhile? I read this interview in which a poet said her mother was senile, but still graced the place by her presence. Sim's like that. She's the kind who can nibble home-made snacks when she goes visiting and say 'ooh' and 'ah', and everyone feels wonderful.

Poor Maya tries to be useful and gets it in the neck. Sim knows what she wants. She wants security. The Dev thing came out of the blue. Someone will turn up again who wants to look after her, and doesn't mind—widow no issue. Once you start marrying, there's no end to it. Too bad Rishad's only nineteen, and in any case Vimi would scratch Sim's eyes out.

Then there's Ved. Ugh, let's not think about Ved. He told Maya once, he likes to have sex seven days a week. He's the original pig. Dev grumbled sometimes that he didn't pay his share when they went yachting or drove up to Matheran or wherever. But basically guys stick together so Sim didn't get a word in. Ma-in-law loves Ved. He chats her up, politics, the weather. Sim would like to drop him, but then again maybe not. Because of Dev.

ॐ

I've told them to come and visit, Sim and Maya that is, but they seem to want to stew. Oh well.

Maya, especially, will now go through her self-flagellation routine. There used to be this whacko who called Maya ten times a day. She'd begin coherently enough and then maunder on about everyone in her family trying to kill her, and Maya would listen because she felt someone should listen. So I said why don't you suggest a counsellor or psychiatrist and she said she did but the woman said the psychiatrist would try to kill her. (Not, if you ask me, a bad idea, but nobody asked me.) Maya wasn't there when she called one day and I said, look, please don't keep ringing, we can't help you, and she said okay and didn't ring again, or only once or twice a day and then stopped.

Maya will learn when she's about a hundred.

৪৩

Maya

I PICKED UP a second-hand copy of *The Egyptian Book of the Dead* at one of these bookshops. I was flipping through it and came across this:

He holdeth fast to the Memory of his identity
In the Great House, and in the House of Fire,
On the dark night of counting all the years,
On the dark nights when months and years are
numbered,
O let my name be given back to me!

When the Divine One on the Eastern Stairs
Shall cause me to sit down with him in peace,
And every God proclaims his name before me,
Let me remember the name I bore!

I don't know why reading that made me cry, right there on the pavement. It was looking at the date I think—3500 BC. Yes, we do all want to be remembered, and remember who we are, even if it was for something bizzare like the longest fingernails ever grown, or losing 900 pounds of weight.

What claims can we make, I wonder, Sim and Dev and Peter and I? Not too many. We are Very Ordinary Bods. Still, we want to be remembered, Sim for her friendship with the Dog with Attitude, Peter for his lasagne verde, me . . . ? Anything will do. Take your pick.

Sim said that on the day before he died Dev had said, 'You know Sim, nothing leaves the earth.' She thought of the earth groaning under the weight of the millions and millions whose dust never left the earth. How come the earth doesn't collapse under the weight? Dust into daisy and all that rigmarole, I suppose. Still, it's pretty awesome.

Dev said he would come back as a whirlwind. Sim had smiled. 'Something more laid back, I think,' she had said.

∞

Peter

DEAR MAYA,

I've been reading 'Indian Diaries' of various sorts by British mems who travelled in India or lived in India with their husbands in the eighteenth and nineteenth centuries. What a pity that 'memsahib' has become such a derogatory word! These women were remarkable. Or at least some of them were. There was a woman called Fanny Parkes who was married to a customs officer, and she refused to be a conventional mem. She used to leave her husband at his job and cavort about India, by camel, horse, boat. There's one you'll find familiar, since you hated those formal dinners at my flat. It's a Mrs Elwood who writes that the social gatherings in Bombay 'were the most dull and uncomfortable meetings one can imagine'. Apparently the few ladies present sat silently on sofas 'staring at each other'. And it took five months to reach India by boat!

Luckily it takes only nine hours now. So pack your bags and come. You can cavort as much as you want, though I can't promise to provide a camel. I miss you. Tim and Kate seem to be settling down, at least they got caught up in the Harry Potter film I took them to. Kate wants a broomstick!

You don't mind taking risks, Maya mem. Take this one.

A hug for Sim and a dozen for you,
Peter

☙

I don't know if she knows it, but Maya has a deep feeling for England. It's drawn from *The French Lieutenant's Woman* and *Chariots of Fire* I tell her. The cool, aristocratic manner, nonchalance about heavy matters. I used to tease her about her fantasies of upper-class Englishmen, and she said no, it's not that really, but a self-possession I don't have and may never have. She told me about a time when she was travelling by tube, and two West Indian women got into a fist-fight. Nobody turned to look at them, they just went on reading their newspapers or hanging on to the straps. It makes ordinary life easier, she says, more civilized, and most of life is ordinary life. It annoyed her when she said please or thank you and people in India said 'Don't be formal'.

She was intrigued while she stayed with friends in a Wiltshire village that people actually had long discussions about whether to start lighting fires in late September or early October, or plan for an early lunch so that they could walk down to a home ten minutes away. It was like living in a Trollope world she said, Anthony, not Joanna. She knows all about contemporary England, of course, and doesn't like it much, and doesn't know whether to laugh or be furious at the vulgar display of an Indian film star's bedroom as part of the India season in London. It's difficult to convince her that expensive kitsch doesn't have to be part of our lives. It's not just that, of course. It's just Maya, tying herself into knots.

Sim is a much easier person, but I don't want to marry Sim, lovely though she is. Dear Maya. Funny old Maya. Utterly maddening Maya. I don't know what will happen in the end, but I'm hoping for the best.

ఇ

Maya

I REMEMBER READING a review once in which the reviewer complained that the novel he was reading did not have a beginning, a middle and an end. He had been taught that novels should have a beginning, a middle and an end, and he felt cheated. I know what he means. I like life in tidy parcels too.

Endings. I contemplate mine in quite a practical way. I must throw out the rubbish in the loft and in the suitcases under the bed and buy new knickers and return books I've borrowed. Do I want to live till I'm two hundred and look like something pickled in formaldehyde? No. But I don't want to end either. I don't want anyone to end. I don't want to contemplate endings.

How did Dev take his dying so calmly? Simran says she doesn't know. Peter says he doesn't know. And I can't ask Dev's mother who will only give me one of her Patient Smiles. Reverend Mother at school used to tell the Christian girls they would understand everything in Heaven. Bully for them, but what happens to the rest of us?

Beginnings. Did birds begin as small, feathered dinosaurs? Did the world begin with a bang? Do you remember Tristram Shandy who had such difficulty deciding where to begin while writing his *Life and Opinions*? To understand him, he felt the reader should know about his parents, his father's brother Toby who lived with them, the batman who tried to protect Uncle Toby from the Widow Wadman who was pursuing him, the doctor who attended on his birth, the carriage he came in, and etc. Three quarters of the way through the book and poor Tristram isn't even born.

I can't afford to talk. Here I am digressing and progressing like Tristram. Is it possible to recapture a person, a life? Especially one that is/was dear.

As for middles, where we are now, the less said the better. Turn on the news. I'm not going to do all your work for you.

இ

I want Time to stop. No. I want it to go backwards. I want to reclaim all those cousins, aunts, uncles who meant so little to me at the time but have left a gap by their going. What is it Anne Ridler says in that poem?—'For it is we who haunt the dead . . .'

The world's no longer familiar. All that eating and drinking, marrying and giving in marriage, all that catching a bus, a train, to rush to a job, it seems surreal. Peter says it's some kind of delayed reaction to everything, Dev and all. But I don't know. Sim says I can't save the world if it doesn't want to be saved. Deblina says I want to play Gawd, and I should bitch sometimes. Apparently it does wonders for the soul. I told Deblina that I'd go shopping, that might help. She e-mailed back, 'And you'll buy stuff you don't want from shops that you think are unsuccessful.'

My God, am I as dreary as that?

Sim floats along. I went to see her the other day and she didn't ask 'Vodka with Schweppes?' She just fixed it and brought it to me. 'Cheers, Maya,' she said and I said 'Cheers, Simran.'

I don't know how she does it.

෴

Simran

How do I cope, Maya wants to know. How did I cope with marriage? How did I cope with the death of a child and a husband? How do I cope? Period. Poor Dev, coping with infinity, the tedium of it.

Maya would like to marry, not because she really wants to, but just for the experience. She envies the elderly couples she sees, who seem so at peace with each other. She feels strongly about women's rights, but throwaway marriages appal her. What can I tell her? We managed, somehow, Dev and I. Would things have changed, for better or worse, had we been given another ten years together? Would it have worked better if I had married some other guy?

Who's to tell?

∞